ADVANCE PRAISE

"No one writes body horror better than R.A. Busby. This book had me shuddering, in full-on cringe mode, wanting to get in the shower and scrub my skin off as I checked every crease of my body for mysterious growths. But this book is more than just its incredibly visceral scenes of shock and disgust. It is also emotional, connecting you to the raw pain and grief of the characters. You suffer with them, become one with them — almost as if you're part of a mycelial network. An absolutely unforgettable book."

Jill Girardi, Author and Owner of Kandisha Press

"I was captivated by *You Will Speak For The Dead* and its lyrical examination of loss and connectedness. It was poignant, with just the right touches of humor and ick, and so well written that I could feel the words — sensations, scents, emotions. I loved this novella and I'll be thinking about it for a long time."

Zoje Stage, USA Today bestselling author of *Baby Teeth* and *Dear Hanna*

"*You Will Speak For The Dead* is that rare kind of story, the kind that pulls you in immediately with an intriguing premise and pitch perfect pacing. Busby's authorial voice is both striking and accessible, and her gift for empathetic characters and situations is unparalleled. Equal parts poignant and disturbing, thought provoking and revolting, the overall experience is so much more than the sum of its parts. Wonderful."

Laurel Hightower, author of *Crossroads* and *The Day of the Door*

You Will Speak For The Dead

This is a work of fiction, and any errors of scientific or academic understanding are the author's. Characters and events in this novella are imaginary, and where locations, events, public figures, or corporations are mentioned, all are used fictitiously with no intended resemblance to a specific person or entity.

You Will Speak For The Dead

Cover design by Selena Middleton

Edited by Selena Middleton

Published by Stelliform Press
Hamilton, Ontario, Canada
www.stelliform.press

Library and Archives Canada Cataloguing in Publication
Title: You will speak for the dead / R.A. Busby. Names: Busby, R. A., author.
Identifiers: Canadiana (print) 20240391276 | Canadiana (ebook) 20240391284
| ISBN 9781738316595 (softcover) | ISBN 9781998466009 (EPUB)
Subjects: LCGFT: Novels. Classification: LCC PS3602.U878 Y68 2024 |
DDC 813/.6—dc23

To Louis, hopeful green grass, smallest sprout,
deepest root, and lasting flower.

YOU WILL SPEAK FOR THE DEAD

R.A. BUSBY

Stelliform Press
Hamilton, Ontario

I

All human things are subject to decay.

John Dryden

I used to clean hoarder houses.

If you heard the term "hoarding" before the TV show made it part of the American vocabulary, you may have thought it was some rare aberration. Perhaps you first heard it called Collyer's Syndrome after the famously wealthy, famously reclusive brothers crushed to death in their luxurious Harlem brownstone beneath the weight of their own possessions, a looming tower that included fourteen pianos, jars of pickled human organs, a functional X-ray machine, and 25,000 books.

For reasons you'll come to understand, I've thought a lot about those brothers, about their deaths, about their stuff. Was this just runaway greed? Untreated mental illness? An ironically appropriate metaphor for capitalism? I didn't know. Mostly I was just sorry for those brothers, for their isolation. Even though they lived in the same apartment, something tells me each one died alone.

Despite my former job, I can't tell you why we hoard things. I'm no psychiatrist — hell, I didn't even finish my college degree — but I suspect at some deep primal level, it's about survival. Squirrels hoard, of course, and so do desert packrats, whose syrupy urine acts like amber to preserve seeds, plants, and wood in middens lasting for thousands of years, a detailed botanical record of the ancient past preserved in rodent pee. In college, my roommate low-key suspected me of stealing his lighters until the day he opened a storage cabinet to find his pet ferret had been the real culprit all along. She'd stashed hundreds of them, lining them up along the cabinet walls with every metal head pointed in the same direction. Why did she keep them? Nobody knew. She couldn't even smoke.

Not long after I started doing cleanouts, I realized my mother had probably been a hoarder. An organized hoarder, yes, but a hoarder, her various collections stashed in labeled Sterilite bins each facing the same way. She and the ferret would have understood each other. Some of her collections made sense, like boxes of family photographs and old letters, but much of what Mom kept seemed just plain weird to me. Why keep bags of aluminum pull-tabs or every HBO Guide from 1981 to 1995? At least I found out from Derek that those were worth something, which I guess makes our relationship not a complete failure.

What I do know is this: It's hard to let things go.

Derek and I met after Mom died, when Pete and I were cleaning out her house. Her death came as a shock to my brother and me, and to be honest, we put off dealing with her stuff until we couldn't anymore. I brought a bunch of landscaping bags, and Peter rented a dumpster, but the job proved harder than either of us had anticipated. Even emptying weeks-old kitchen garbage felt like throwing out my mom in little bits.

Deep in her closet, I unearthed a ragged flannel shirt she'd kept back there for decades. I found it tucked behind a tie-dyed tee Pete and I had made for her one summer in Vacation Bible School, but I'd never seen her wear that flannel one. Had it belonged to our father? To hers? By then, it was too late to ask. I stood with the damn thing in my hand until my sister-in-law gently wrapped her arm around my shoulders and said, "You can keep it if you want, Paul, but ask yourself if it's your memories you're keeping, or hers." At this, I broke down and let the shirt go into the dumpster.

I never forgot about it, though.

Yes, it's hard to let go. More than almost anything else, I think that moment is the reason I understood so much about the final hoarder house I ever cleaned, the old professor's place at 982 Avirosa Avenue.

II

I bequeath myself to the dirt to grow from the grass I love.
If you want me again, look for me under your boot-soles.

Walt Whitman

When I first saw 982 Avirosa Avenue, I thought the place looked bad. Even from the curb, I could tell the house was a Level 4 cleanup at least. Dirt dimmed the formerly-white siding; shingles had blown down, and the worst sign was this: though the house was a small two-bedroom, we'd needed a forty-yard rollaway dumpster, the biggest we could get.

Shit.

"Right here, Paul." Imani gestured to a mailbox nearly hidden by Bermuda grass the color of old hay.

I'd been with Junkitt about a year when it happened. Until recently, they'd been my biggest rival. They were a three-person fringe business like mine, and for months we'd been in fierce competition for housecleaning jobs until I got a text from Imani, the Junkitt founder, proposing what amounted to a merger. She came to the bargaining table with PPE, respirators, and two heavy lifters consisting of a dude named Kevin and a green-haired powerhouse named Elisa. I came with two hands, a bow rake, a ShopVac, some Tyvek suits, and a working truck. We struck a deal.

I pulled up next to the forty-yard and yanked the parking brake. "All right, folks," Imani called to the back. "Let's get to it. There's a lot."

When we'd all assembled, Imani briefed us. "The client's the one who called," she said. "He's the homeowner, but his sister-in-law's the one who actually lives here. Used to work as a professor of bio research at the university, but — well, she's not doing so hot now. Balance issues. Forgetting things. Losing track of time. The usual."

Kevin frowned. "She live by herself? No adult kids or anything?"

"Doesn't look like it." Imani flipped over a sheet on her clipboard. "From what I gathered, she kinda keeps to herself, not many ties to other folks. The client mentioned there's no one to care for her, so he's moving her into assisted living."

Kevin snorted. "Out of sight, out of mind, I guess. Bye, grandma, and thanks for all the cookies."

"Where's the old lady at, anyway?" asked Elisa, peering at the house.

"Visiting relatives back East." Imani circled something on the second page. "He's going to be turning the house into a rental, if I had to guess. Either way, he needs the place cleaned before Thursday so he can get her living arrangements squared away before she comes back."

"And he wants all her shit thrown out? He doesn't want to save *nothin'*?" Elisa shook her head. "Damn. Ain't even his stuff, is it? What if there's some, you know, valuable microscopes and shit?" She paused a minute, idly kicking at an empty soda can embedded in the powdery dirt. "Hey, um. If we see something we like, can we ... you know, take it? I mean, the owner don't give a fuck. Just going in the landfill, right?"

Imani looked down at the contract on the clipboard, then nodded. "You see something worth saving, set it aside. We'll talk to the guy." But from the way she said it, I got the feeling this client didn't want to deal with too many follow-up questions.

I have a theory that the first hoarder piles begin as junk mail. You know, a handful of coupons and sales promos you tossed on the kitchen table and saved because they could be useful. Soon, the coupons get buried under a magazine subscription you never got around to canceling and a few bills you're afraid to look at.

From there, proto-piles start springing up in corners like mushrooms after rain. A mismatched shoe. The cans you intended to recycle because you didn't want to add to the landfill and they didn't do curbside. Those VHS tapes of *Who Wants to Be a Millionaire?* Junk, right? Sure. But it's *your* junk. And the longer you let the junk stay, the harder it is to let go.

I didn't get it at first, not until I remembered Mom's flannel shirt, the frayed seams of the shoulders, the way the fabric smelled a bit like her. When I told Pete I felt guilty about throwing it away, my brother had been more sanguine. "You can't keep everything, right?" he'd said, and scooped Mom's dusty jars of spices into a garbage bag.

But what if you *could?*

There's a profound reassurance in the permanent mountain of stuff. Through the decades, the pile abides, adding layer upon layer like a packrat midden, impervious to change or transition or trauma. Your mother may die. The love of your life may move away to Vancouver and never call you anymore. Cancer, coronaries, Covid, or cholesterol may claim your family and friends, but throughout this turmoil the pile remains, year after year, decade after decade, a stable point in a swiftly turning world. Nothing is ever lost. The pile preserves everything intact.

Can you imagine it? The stability? The peace?

Think for a minute. Where's your senior yearbook? How about the stocking your mom hung over the fireplace every Christmas, or the blue leather collar from the good, sweet dog you last saw the day you took him to the vet and held him close till he was all done living?

Where did it go?

No worries. It's in the pile. It's all right there below your hands. When someone leaves or dies, we say we lost them, but in the pile, nothing is lost. These things will never leave you, never abandon you, never die. The pile isn't going anywhere.

You see, most folks hoard for one big reason: a response to major trauma. Every hoard, like every human, is unique.

And each one is a monument to loss.

That's why the thought of this biology professor lady coming back from a visit and finding we'd cleaned out her whole life didn't sit quite well with me at all. No. Not at all.

"Oh, shit," muttered Imani as we wedged our way inside. Even when unlocked, the front door had been immovable, but when we tried the back, Elisa and Kevin managed to wrench the sliding-glass door open just enough for us to shoulder in sideways. Inside, the house was too dark to make out a goddamned thing.

Elisa yanked at a crumbling curtain which fell apart in her hand. Through the mottled dust came a faint yellow light. Now we could see what we were in for. Sort of.

The first object I spotted happened to be a Sterilite container, and I'll tell you, it gave me a bit of a shock. This one hadn't been stuffed with old HBO guides or aluminum pull-tabs, though, just Christmas ornaments. An old wooden nutcracker in there bared his teeth as he gnashed through a sea of red balls, while beside the container, a child's blue stool lay with its legs to the ceiling like a dead bug. Overhead, books on swaybacked shelves leaned on each other like drunks, and as I walked past, one fell at my feet, a volume titled *Taxonomy of Fungi Imperfecti*, its pages swelled and curled from water damage.

"Kevin?" I called. "We probably want to watch out for mold. You got your mask on?"

"Yeah. Too bad mold's the least of our problems."

Over everything lay a fine white dust. I rubbed the powder between my fingers, expecting it to feel like fine beach sand, but it was feathery and warm, like snow turned to down.

"What the hell is this stuff?" Kevin asked, trying to shake the powder off his palm. "You think the ceiling's okay?"

Elisa peered up at some brownish staining. "Ceiling, yeah, but overall, I think this house is probably fucked," she said. "Ducts are dirtier than an asshole."

Our feet plowed through that odd powder, leaving crisp prints behind us like the ones the astronauts made on the moon. I'd read that those prints would remain there unchanged for millions of years, long after time erased all things made by humans. I stared back at the print I'd left in the powder. By the end of the day, it had vanished.

The rust-colored carpet sank uneasily beneath our feet as Kevin and the others tried to clear a working path for our equipment.

"Step carefully," Imani warned. "Kevin, keep your mask on over your nose. Something tells me the refrigerator is going to be a serious health hazard. Do we have the heavy contractors' bags for that?"

"Yeah, and we're sure as shit gonna need them." Kevin shook his head. "You smell this place?"

I did. At first, the scent reminded me of perfume, honeyish, like baby powder or jasmine gone a little rank. Then the odor deepened, became sultry, took on a waxiness like blue cheese dripping with sugar. Then the gangrenous miasma hit me. My mask filled with it, and I braced myself against my knees, trying hard not to hurl.

"Open the windows," Imani called, but Kevin was already high-stepping over the piles by the entrance.

"Place is a firetrap," he shouted, his voice muffled. "Nobody light the stove, all right? Not like you would, but I'm just saying. Lemme get the respirators as soon as I get this door —" He grunted, shoving away a metal bed frame. "— fuckin' open. Smells like ass in here."

Shameless now, I bolted for the sliding glass door behind me, my hip slamming into a table along the way, and made it to the door barely in time to yank my mask aside. My breakfast of coffee and Danish had soured in my stomach, and now, clinging to the rusted remains of a porch pillar, I vomited into the overgrown bushes of ragged desert broom growing wild at the side of the house.

"Hey, Paul, why don'tcha do your hurling inside?" called Kevin genially. "Probably make the place smell better."

My laugh came out along with some more puke. After another twisting heave, I spat a string of yellow bile into the desert broom and ran my hands across my face, feeling the touch of the white powder from the house clinging to my nose.

11

Inside, Elisa handed me a pocket-sized jar of Vicks, an idea she'd gotten from watching *Silence of the Lambs* about a million times. Taking a judicious swipe, I stuck my finger under my N-95 to smear the salve beneath my nostrils. Hell, I smeared it *inside* my nostrils for good measure, not giving a shit about the sting.

"Careful how you step." Elisa nodded. "Stick to the floor joists, Paul. If you punch through, Imani might put you on fridge cleanout duty, and that shit's gonna be baaaad. Anyone know if this place has a basement?"

At my feet, I heard a little tinking sound. I bent, careful of the squishy flooring, and spotted a tiny antique teacup, a pink thing with a gold-plated handle. A collector's item, perhaps, the kind you see in old ladies' china cabinets or undusted antique shops. Before he'd left me and moved to Vancouver, Derek had taught me a few tips about porcelain, and I flipped the cup over to examine the bottom for a maker's mark, but I could only make out the letter "m" and a shape vaguely resembling a mushroom.

Turning it back over, I burst into a chuckle. Beside the gold handle, a picture-perfect painted hedgehog stared out at me defiantly, his small black eyes glimmering above a pointed, pugnacious nose. He stood on a tuft of grass amidst a scatter of fallen leaves, poised as if ready to scamper at any moment. Below him in flowing copperplate was the name "Jack Sharpnails." Perfect.

I cradled the cup in my hand, caught by those tough little eyes, then looked at it again. At first, the hedgehog's expression had seemed wary and wild, but now I saw something more like pleading. Loneliness. A sense of betrayal for being thrown away like so much trash when it had done nothing wrong.

I blinked.

Carefully, I found a place for Jack Sharpnails on a side table, a refuge half-hidden by the overhang of the kitchen counter where he could be safe. Then I looked for his matching saucer, overturning stacks of magazines and trying not to step too hard in case I found it with my feet, but it never turned up. Before I left that first day, I touched the cup's gold handle one more time. You understand. Just to be sure.

It began with that Jack Sharpnails cup, I'm sure of it. I couldn't let him go, you see, couldn't let him die. I should've known it wasn't going to end there.

And it didn't.

III

It is the secret of the world that all things subsist and do not die,
but only retire a little from sight and afterward return again.

Ralph Waldo Emerson

Let's talk about loss.

You remember your soul doll? You know the one I mean.
Maybe it was a teddy, a blankie, a dinosaur, or an actual doll. But
no matter what, you took it everywhere, slept beside it, told it all
your secrets. Because it held your heart, it never whispered a word
to another living soul. This was your personal Velveteen Rabbit,
the toy which was Alive.

Yeah. I think you know the one I mean.

Mine actually *was* a velveteen rabbit, imaginatively named
Hoppy. By the time I buried him, his fur had worn away to nothing, and his eyes had fallen off. When I tried to replace them by
gluing circles of construction paper to the ruins of his good, sweet
face, bits of stuffing spilled out from the worn places in his fabric
and fell into my lap like dry white tears.

I hadn't meant to bury him. I'd only been playing.

14

Visiting our grandparents one summer in Maine, we'd all gone to the beach, my mother, my brother Peter, and me. The day began sunny before turning cold, but all the while, the water stayed a perfect navy blue. By the time I'd walked up and down the shoreline, staring at the mussels on the rocks, my feet had gone grayish and wrinkled from the chill. I buried my toes deep into the warm sand, and thinking Hoppy might also be cold, I buried him there too. Then Peter found a tiny crab who snapped at us with its business claw, so we took turns poking the crab with a discarded popsicle stick, hoping it would grab ahold so we could take it home and keep it. Then Mom called us to get ice cream, and it was only when I woke up at three in the morning that I remembered him, my rabbit in the sand.

"We'll get him tomorrow," my mother reassured me, her eyes swollen from being awakened from a sound sleep by my frantic wailing. "No, Paulie. We can't go right now. It's too dark to see him. Hoppy will be there in the morning."

But he wasn't.

In the years that passed, I was occasionally struck by a vast and crushing wave of guilt at the thought of Hoppy waiting patiently beneath the sand, hoping I would come and dig him out. He had been a good rabbit, the best rabbit, but I'd never come back.

"Oh, fuck me," said Kevin from the master bedroom.

We'd been at it for hours by the time we worked ourselves back there, and Kevin had been the first one inside the room.

"No one's gonna fuck you, Kevin," said Elisa. Through the green hair falling over her face, she shot me a wink as I passed, and I smiled, even though she couldn't see it underneath my mask.

"And if they did, you'd never shut up about it."

Kevin waved a hand at her. "I mean it, guys. Look at this shit."

Initially, the master bedroom had been almost completely dark, an impassable maze of books stacked in piles halfway to the ceiling. Some were ones you'd actually read — your Stephen Kings, your Diana Gabaldons, your Michael Crichtons — but most came with titles I couldn't even pronounce, much less understand. *Trichlomas of North America. Ascomycete Fungi of North America.* Real page-turners. Beside me lay a volume called *North American Boletes,* and for variety on the other side, *The Boletes of North America.* The only one I kinda-sorta understood was *How to Know Gilled Mushrooms,* but then I realized it wasn't a backyard cookbook.

Kevin yanked at the curtain until it fell away with a sad little purr. Then the light flooded in, and I saw what he'd been swearing about.

"Oh, fuck me," I said.

The mushrooms were growing everywhere.

On the bed, the floor, in a tidy little stack up the corner of one wall, every surface teemed with clustered mushrooms. Brown mushrooms flowered behind the door like pleated circles of brown leather. A mushroom with a gray frayed edge poked its head through a tiny hole in the plaster. Above me grew a pair of little whitish ones like perfect conical hats dipping flirtatiously from the ceiling.

Kevin nodded at me. He was a bulky, potatoish guy, his face a series of circles, and now his green eyes, always a little large, seemed to bulge above the margin of his mask while he took in the extent of the job. "Christ. You ever seen anything like this, Paul?"

I shook my head. "No. Not ever. You?"

"In this fucking desert? Naah. House mushrooms are more of a back-East thing, I think. Only mushrooms I've seen in Vegas were growing in dog shit."

"I got news for ya," Elisa said to both of us, a half-smile push-ing at one side of her mask. "You know the carpet we've been walking on? The kinda spongy, rust-colored stuff everywhere in the living room?"

"Yeah?" Kevin returned.

"It ain't carpet."

"Oh, FUCK me." Grunting, Kevin worked his way around piles of books to the other window and pulled down that curtain too.

The room was a bit humid from the swamp cooler, and I saw the mushrooms mostly grew around book stacks beside the walls and windows, places the house probably leaked. I could see how that would happen.

And as I stared at the mushrooms, I really *did* see. My vision — well, it just shifted. The light changed, the haze of the room clearing away. For a moment, it felt like I'd stepped into a different version of the place, as if the vision were reality and the piles of books and spongy carpet had been a dream of another world. Now, instead of the dry, dusty day outside, rain came draining down the pane as if the glass itself were weeping, or maybe I got that idea from the weeping woman on the bed.

Along the windowpane and down the sill, the water dripped slow splashes on the covers of the books, wetting the pages about boletes and ascomycetes. Looking down, I saw her feet, but they were *my* feet too, sticking out from beneath the covers, our long toes bare and bony, our old woman's feet with cracked heels and painted pink nails.

Beside me, a copy of *A Walk Through the Woods* soaked, swelled, and exploded in a proliferous mushroom bouquet, caps curving in a curl like calla lilies, the flowers of the dead, and it was then I caught a low-pitched murmur as if someone spoke directly in my ear. *No, Paul, they aren't calla lilies, but oysters. Oyster mush-rooms, pleurotus ostreatus, lignin-lovers; they break through lignin in the paper of the books to get to the sweet cellulose.* Soft, dry fingers wove through mine like vines on branches, not just my hand now, but hers too, *ourhand yespaulyes.*

"Paul. Gimme a hand, man," barked Kevin. "Come on, dude, what the fuck."

"Sorry." I blinked, feeling oddly like I'd doubled in time. Sun-beams strained through dusty windows but the panes seemed also to be weeping. The ravaged copy of *A Walk in the Woods* lay not at my feet (*painted pink nails*) but at the foot of the bed where her (*my our*) feet would have been. The book blackened, its pages rotted, and the mushrooms withered and wrinkled into twists of old dull brown. *Lignin,* I thought. *They unwrapped the paper for its cellulose candy.* Yeah. Kevin had said it best. What the fuck?

I stumbled to the corner where Kevin was breaking down the biggest piles of books. He passed me a trash bag, but when he grabbed the first volumes, I heard a heavy *brrrt* sound, and the room filled with a powdery haze like slow-floating cigarette smoke.

"Jesus." I jumped back a bit. "Careful, Kevin, I think it's burn-ing." But it wasn't.

Beneath the books I spotted white-thread filaments woven through the room in all directions, lacing everything, connecting everything, touching everything. In the stack at my feet, the lowest books nearly disappeared in the delicate webwork, words drowned in something like rain-soaked dandelion puff. Only the top layer remained relatively undisturbed, but below, a white spiderweb cottonball wonderland had linked everything in one enormous growth.

"Fuck." I wiped my fingers on my pants, but not successfully. "Is this a root system?"

Kevin shrugged. "Maybe. Or just gross shit. Bottom line, I

don't give a crap what it is. We gotta get it out of here." With that, he handed me a pile of bolete books and told me to throw them out. I did, but every time Kevin peeled away a layer and I caught the heavy, quiet *brrrrt brrrt* of the root system ripping, it almost seemed to hurt.

By quitting time, we'd cleared the main bedroom — now dubbed the Shroom Room — but there remained a ton of work still left to do. Imani and I had known from the start this wouldn't be a one-day job, but even so, this pile seemed bigger on the inside. Elisa offered to treat us to some cold ones at McDermott's, our favorite bar, but I begged off. I felt bone-weary, and I just wanted a bath.

At home, I marched straight to the tub, stripping as I went, but the trail of my discarded clothes reminded me of the piles I'd waded through all day, and in my head, I heard Elisa saying, "You know the spongy stuff? It ain't carpet."

Jesus.

I backtracked and picked up the clothes. Derek would have been so proud of me.

Ironically, hoarder houses were the reason I met Derek. They were also the reason he left me.

After Mom died, Pete hired an estate-sale company to assess her remaining stuff for things they could reasonably expect to sell. At one point, an agent tapped me on the shoulder and asked if he could have a quick peek at some of the items I'd tossed into the giant walk-in dumpster Pete had rented. I said that would be fine. Distracted by watching strangers debate what they could get for my mom's old Mixmaster, I wasn't paying much attention to him. "You'd be surprised," the agent remarked as we headed out the door. "Folks throw out a lot of useful things without even knowing what they're worth."

The dumpster had a side entrance you could walk through, and the agent peered inside. Sure enough, the first thing he grabbed was Mom's old Sterilite box with all those *HBO Guides* faithfully saved from the days of early cable yore. "Yep," the agent said, tapping on the faded label in Mom's neat handwriting. "Here we go. Don't toss these out. You can get twenty bucks for them on eBay, at least."

"Per *box?*" I looked up, really seeing him for the first time. So elegant. God. Dark eyes set in smooth, dark skin, a fashionable silk necktie that matched a colorful pocket square. A tailored suit fitting easily over a slender torso. Abashed, I ducked my head and stared at his fingers. Pale and underwhelming as I was, I'd never considered myself particularly hot, and my attempts at conversation were usually cringeworthy, so I generally avoided looking right at people. A real recipe for success, as I'm sure you'd agree.

The agent shook his head. "No, Mr. Simard. Not twenty dollars per box. Twenty dollars per *guide.*" Then he paused, waiting for me. I looked up, certain he'd be smirking, but he wasn't. In his warm eyes I saw kindness. Compassion. And … interest. "Hey," the agent said. "Is it okay if I call you Paul?"

It was okay. And that's how I met Derek, the love of my life.

As Derek later explained, estate sale companies get calls all the time from grieving, overwhelmed people whose dead parents' houses, full of memories and mess, have made them give up the last of their fucks. At best, death is disruptive and destabilizing, inevitably hitting people when they're in the middle of their jobs, their kids, their lives. We're never ready. We're always doing something when it comes, and when it does, we don't know what to do.

And maybe in the midst of that upheaval, you wonder, *Why*

do anything? Why not just do … nothing? Leave it alone. Keep it all the same. Forever.

"They need help," Derek told me gently. "They need help letting things go."

I could relate.

Whenever the estate sale company received a desperate call for a cleaner, Derek would shoot me a text, and soon I had a little off-label Craigslist and Facebook Marketplace business going. It didn't pay much, but it paid something, and I needed the money. Besides, it wasn't difficult, just an extension of the work Pete and I had done at Mom's.

But soon enough I started getting calls for tougher jobs. Hoarder houses. No, not Level 5 cleanouts so extreme they required special air filters or OSHA-compliant respirators, but the Level 2-4 places ranging from "Grandpa's house is kinda messy" to "For God's sake, don't light any matches."

As there were a ton of those, my one-man business took off. For one, I didn't charge a lot. Junk removal companies typically bill between five and ten dollars a square foot, and that adds up quickly. My fee sat more in the two- to three-buck range, so I got a decent amount of work. I liked it. It felt oddly healing, you know? Cleaning things up. Restoring order. Putting parts of a life back in place.

Derek had been fine with normal cleanups and glad to send some business my way. Until I started taking on the extreme hoarder houses, we'd been a dream team, but after that, our relationship began to die a slow and probably inevitable death. Derek found the hoarder houses damn gross, though he was too polite to say so directly. Instead, I caught it mostly in little things. Flared nostrils.

Turning away when I came in. Moving his hands away before I reached for them.

How could I blame him? My day job featured bathtubs black with grime, scattered bands of roaches, refrigerators dripping sticky brown ooze from wire shelves, plates buried under mounds of greenish mold, and bags and bags of adult diapers, a solution many folks hit on after their bathrooms became too packed to use for, well, bathrooming.

Gradually, Derek began filling our bathroom with soaps, nail brushes, loofahs, expensive shampoo, new washcloths and towels. Sheets got laundered daily. Eventually, I started coming in by the back door so I could dump my clothes straight into the washing machine before I saw him, and though he'd always taken a shower after we made love, he spent more time there now, scrubbing me off his skin. Once you go there in a relationship, it's pretty much over. Our connection slipped apart, like fingers untwining.

We parted amicably, but although he'd promised to keep in touch, he didn't. I moved out, taking my battered truck and our bed, and Derek snagged a job with a ritzier estate sale company in Vancouver. Because I'm pathetic, I googled his company one night when I couldn't sleep. It's a hip, modern place that looks like a cement parking garage strung with bare Edison bulbs and hanging plants. Without Derek, my new apartment seemed too large, my feet too loud, my voice abrasive in the silence, and at night when I stretched out my hand across the bed, no one else reached out to take it.

I hope Derek's doing well. I thought about him a lot back then, probably too often. Even so, I'm glad he didn't see what happened to me in the house on Avirosa.

You see, he ... wouldn't understand. Not at all.

After work, I lay back in the steaming bath, muscles easing one by one, the events of the day seeping out of me into the water. My hair still smelled of puke, and my nose was clogged from that white powder drifting over everything in the old woman's house. Even the steam of the bathwater rising in a curling mist reminded me of the smoke I'd seen drifting up from the piles of books Kevin pulled apart in the Shroom Room. It hadn't been smoke, though. Probably dust.

It wasn't dust. I know better now.

We know better now.

Like most people, I'd only known one thing about mushrooms: Unless they came from the produce section, they were deadly poison. I'd eaten mushrooms in salads and pizza; I'd used the red-and-white kind to power up in Mario Kart, but that was about all. In college, a friend gave me about two or three grams of the fun kind before a Twenty One Pilots concert, and since I'd heard people claiming they let your consciousness penetrate the interconnected life of the universe or whatever, I took them. I still remember the flavor, earthy and bitter like hay-flavored pasta, but they didn't do much besides make me vaguely nauseated. The band was great, though.

In any case, the dust I'd seen hadn't been smoke, but spores. Spores spill from fruiting fungi to drift along the currents of the air like swooping swallows before they land and find a place to grow. They are so oddly beautiful.

What you may not know is this. Take a breath. Go ahead. Really.

You just inhaled a few.

No big deal? Maybe. If you ever scratched your way through athlete's foot or a bad yeast infection, though, I'm guessing you're not on Team Fungus, and every kid from Arizona knows valley fever is a thing. Sure, our immune systems will try to defend us, but as of late … well, they're struggling. Times are changing.

And speaking of time, I wonder what we'll do when the permafrost thaws. When the wind begins to blow and dries the soil. When it sweeps across clusters of spores that haven't taken a trip in the breeze since the last mammoth died.

By the way, you just inhaled some more.

Drying myself, I noticed something had changed.

For a long while I lay in the bath limp as a teabag until the rank rot smell diminished, but when my skin began to wrinkle, I gave in and reached for a towel. Beneath my fingers, my flesh felt oddly swollen, even stiff. Outside my job, I wasn't much of a gym rat, but now I flashed on memories of post-workout leg day, the muscles puffy and taut. Still, not even after my best workouts had my skin ever … *crackled.* As I ran my fingertips down my quads, something in there felt like half-defrosted chicken, almost crispy. When I bent down, I spotted something growing on my foot.

Tucked between my first and second toes — and the third and fourth ones on my other foot — I saw a delicate dusting like mud, but it wasn't. I'd soaked in the bath for half an hour at least, my feet underwater the whole time. I poked the mud dusting and found it soft, almost spongy. And it was growing on me.

What had Elisa said? *It ain't carpet.*

Shit.

Okay, I confess to a few occasions of dudebath mentality. *I don't need to scrub down there. I'm getting water on it, aren't I? Who's really got time to wash their legs? Besides, the runoff from my shampoo will take care of it.* Derek had not been amused, and to be honest, he'd been right. Lathering up a scrubby bath cloth thing, I started powerwashing every damn crack I possessed. Fingers. Butt cheeks.

24

Armpits. All around my dick. And yeah, up and down my legs and between my toes.

But there was something else. When I scrubbed lower down, the washcloth thing came away covered in white filaments. At first, I thought it was just lather. I spread the cloth open on the side of the tub to see better, and my first thought after *candy it's cotton candy* was that I'd grabbed a handful of spiderwebs.

But the spiderweb filaments had come from behind my balls. They had been growing there.

Twenty minutes later, I ventured out of the bath again, rubbing each surface of my skin with the roughest towel I owned, one Derek had dubbed The Exfoliator. I was pink as a baby; my skin actually shone. I felt reborn.

The next morning, I woke up feeling exhausted and foolish. My room was a disaster. On the floor lay piles of wet towels from last night's stupid freakout about dirt I hadn't washed off in the bathtub. Obviously I was a human troll, and Derek had been right to leave me.

Worse, I'd slept like crap. My dreams had featured a rotating slideshow of disturbing images: A dark doorway hidden by bushes. A black cave of groaning metal verging on collapse. A white webwork glowing with an eerie, eldritch light. Above it all, the sickly smell of death. When I jerked awake at three in the morning, I found I'd been crying.

It was the damned Jack Sharpnails cup. I couldn't stop thinking about his round black eyes, those tiny-shiny eyes that glared at me in fury when I'd put him aside and left him to his fate at the bottom of a dumpster. Whoever in that house had cared for him, treasured him, it didn't matter. I'd been his last real hope. He'd been a good boy on a good cup, and I'd just put him down and walked away.

Lonely, I thought. So damn lonely.

I told myself this whole thing was stupid, that I'd acquired some weird fixation, that I had turned into my college roommate's ferret. *No, Paul,* I scolded myself. *It's too dark right now. The cup will be there in the morning.*

Five minutes later, I was driving back to Avirosa Avenue.

Wedging myself through the sliding glass door, the smell of the empty house hit me again. I'd forgotten to wear my mask. Shooting a baleful look at the refrigerator, which we hadn't gotten to yet, I could only imagine what horrors lay within. Expired chicken, maybe. Thanksgiving turkey the color of ripe blue cheese. Gravy from Satan's bunghole. Who knows?

I set about to find the little cup.

For a few ugly minutes, I couldn't find the place I'd put him down. I scrabbled through the pile at my feet, but nothing remained but paper scraps on the squishy fungal carpet.

My breathing grew harsher, and I stopped, willing myself to follow the advice Mom had given me and Peter if we ever got lost: stop walking, look around, and get oriented.

With the door left open, the stench had dissipated, and in the peace of early dawn, nothing moved, nothing stirred. Beneath my feet I sensed a subtle vibration, a deep, low pitch almost like a rolling wave.

Still, no matter where I looked, I couldn't find that little hedgehog cup.

The problem was this: Everything in the house looked different now. We'd hauled away so many of the piles that the physical configuration of the interior had totally changed, and I no longer knew where things had been.

A professor from one of my first (and final) college classes had a theory about place memory. We all made it here, she said, in part because our ancestors recalled where they had found ripe hazelnuts, or trees that still bore fruit, or fallen logs with mushrooms you could eat more than once. Memories, she said, are bound up with location. Remembering that, I wondered if a hoarder's piles helped them to keep their bearings. A space of permanence and order in a world composed of too much pain and loss. Too much destruction. Cliffs tumbling into the sea. Fires creeping down a mountain like dark orange lace, forests of trees turned to standing black toothpicks.

In such a whirlwind, how could we remember who we were? Where we'd been?

And where the hell had that stupid cup gone?

I covered my face and looked not with my eyes, but with my memory. A ghostly Elisa warned me to watch where I stepped; Kevin tromped around like a bull, high-stepping over piles, and in my nose hung the cloying stench of rot and mold overlaid by the sharp bite of Vicks.

Then just like that, I knew exactly where I'd laid the little cup. Eyes still closed, I turned to the side table beneath the countertop. I had put Jack Sharpnails there, and then I'd touched the graceful gold handle to be sure he was safe.

I opened my eyes. The side table had been taken out. Nothing looked the same. Fuck.

And then, behind a broken pot on the kitchen counter, I saw a glint of gold. The graceful, gilded handle. When the cup lay in my hand, I felt relief so powerful I had to stop to breathe. My god.

Cradling the cup, I turned it over as I had before and saw the wild, dark eyes of the hedgehog staring back, the swooping

27

copperplate cursive reading "Jack Sharpnails." He glared at me reproachfully.

"I'm sorry for leaving you," I whispered. "I'm sorry I left you. I'm sorry."

IV

Where there is too much, there is not enough.

Proverb

By the time the others arrived, I'd been hard at work for hours. Imani drove the truck, expertly three-pointing on the narrow street, and when she got out, she teased me for being early. I handed her a cup of coffee I'd picked up about a half hour before they arrived, and that was all good. Elisa and Kevin entered on a wave of laughter and raucous music, and that felt all good too.

But later, when I went to the truck to get my lunch and tried to pull off the gloves I'd been wearing, they straight-up stuck to my skin. For a second, I stared at them stupidly, wondering if Kevin or Elisa had pulled some practical joke on me — "*Let's put Superglue in his gloves and see if he figures it out!*" — but honestly, that wasn't their style.

Pulling my mask aside, I nipped the tip of a middle glove finger with my teeth and withdrew my hand with a decisive yank. The pain shocked through me, immediate and silver as current.

You ever been waxed? Remember that ripping wave like a

million tiny hairs bursting into flame below your skin? I didn't scream, but I drew in a breath, then another, trying to ignore that my upper lip had gone damp with the sweat of shock.

With my glove removed, I confirmed what I'd felt: Across the back of my hand grew a webwork white as snow, a net thin and fine as a fishnet glove. Tiny blood-drops oozed and beaded on the delicate threads. The webwork sprouted from my hand, its pathways following the tracery of my veins, only it wasn't threads I saw.

It looked like roots.

And when I peered into the rearview mirror of the truck, I spotted something else.

In the precise spot I'd touched my nose the day I'd lost my breakfast in the bushes, something was growing. Not a wart, but a spike, thin as a Q-tip, rooted in the corner where my left nostril met my cheek. It looked like a tiny human carrot made of skin.

Running my hands over my face, I found two more skin carrots tucked into my hair above my eyebrow, and another growing on the upper curve of my right ear. The human root reminded me of three or four grains of rice stuck together and embedded in my flesh, the tip curving up in an insouciant little flip. If I arranged my side hair and pinned it down with the strap of my face mask, I could hide it — but for how long? What if the skin carrot blew up to fucking parsnip size? What would I do then? Say *"Yeah, sorry about this head parsnip, guys. It's all the rage on TikTok"*?

I sat in the truck a long time with a rag wrapped around my hand and waited till the pin-sized holes stopped their bleeding. Then you know what? I shoved the glove on and went back to work, that's what. Life had taught me if you ignore a painful thing, it goes away.

Mostly.

Inside, I waited until everyone had wandered off. Imani had gone to the 7-11 for soda, and Elisa and Kevin sat out back eating lunch. They'd be okay if I joined them, but they'd also be okay if I didn't. In the interim, I wanted to check something.

With no one around, I removed the glove again, pulling it off gingerly this time. Running my fingers over the white dust on everything, that warm, powdery deposit (*spores from the asci in the fruiting bodies, they're spores, they're spores, i am a fruiting body so are you paul so are you*), I sensed a subtle thrumming I'd only faintly heard before in the quiet morning. That's the only way I can describe it — a tangible sound like a low hum, an electric vibration through my bones, through the threads of the

mycelium it's called a mycelium a mycelial network

the rootlike system underneath my skin. As I ran my fingers over it, the roots themselves seemed to tangle, interweave, link, connect, and join inside my flesh like they were knitting together. My breath came faster. I found the sensation mesmerizing.

When Elisa came in, I motioned her to one of the piles. "Hey," I asked. "You got a minute? Can you feel anything in here?" Elisa's gloves were on, I noticed with relief. If I'd caught some kind of spore in here, I didn't want her to catch it too. Something told me she would not be happy with skin carrots.

"I'm not feeling *you*, if that's what you're asking," Elisa retorted, but then put her hand on the pile and let it rest there a good few seconds. "Oh, yeah. I can feel something, all right." She nodded, her eyes growing dreamy. "It feels exactly like …"

"What? What does it feel like?"

"Like your mama's big titties," she laughed. Then she said all she really felt was a bunch of old shit that needed taking to the dumpster, and maybe I should lay off the crack sometime.

This was oddly reassuring.

31

After Elisa left, I touched the pile again. Instantly the thrum sprang through my fingertips almost joyfully, and I thought of a symphony orchestra, each sound distinct but interweaving through the whole they made together. If this thrumming vibration had a sound, it would be like the deep murmur of the subsurface of the earth, the mutter of rocks shifting and clashing, the soft sound of rootgrowth in soil. So beautiful. And so alive with memory.

Yes. The memories in the house were very much alive.

"Yep," said Imani, staring into the back bedroom. "There's almost always one room they keep kinda picked up. Guess this is your lucky day, Paul."

I'd expected the back bedroom to be like the rest of the house — bursting with boxes, Sterilite containers, weblike fungus, water-logged editions of *The Mushroom Book of Mushrooms* (*fruiting bodies paul*) or plain old trash, but I'd been wrong. The room had been kept shockingly neat, all things considered. Tidily stacked along one wall were a few cardboard boxes labeled "Drawings," "Memorabilia," and "Toys," but not much else.

Clearly, the room had once belonged to some 90s kid, a teenager who'd tacked up posters of Hootie and the Blowfish and Beck and Smashing Pumpkins interspersed with snapshot collages of himself and his friends doing 90s Kid things. A bunch of teenagers waiting in the ticket line for a Nirvana concert in December of '93. A summertime pool party where 90s Kid wore pool shoes shaped like sharks. At the bottom, 90s Kid stood awkwardly in his graduation robes, the banner behind him reading "CLASS OF '95 4-EVAH!" which meant this dudebro was technically old enough to have been my dad.

It was the contact I noticed most, though. The touch. The

connections. In every picture, the kid was hugging someone, hold-ing hands, flopping his arm across the shoulders and backs of his friends. His face beamed from a bouquet of faces topped by square blue graduation caps, the name John-something on his diploma partly cut off by the frame.

In so many of his pictures, I saw the same older woman. Her hair tumbled down all curly and wild, the kind of hair that silvers in the light like Christmas tinsel. She wasn't pretty, not exactly, but when she smiled, as she did often in these photos, a light shone in her eyes that made me catch my breath. It made her transcen-dent and beautiful, and the pure joy shared between the faces of the woman and the boy shone out so clear that anyone could see he was her son and she loved him.

Anyone could see that. Anyone.

After moving a few boxes, though, I wondered something. The woman had kept graduation pictures and the pool-party sum-mer fun pictures, but where had she put the *other* ones? Besides these snapshots, I'd seen a few little-kid photos in the corridor, three or four baby pictures in the Shroom Room, but what about the rest? Besides Newborn John and Graduate John (CLASS OF '95 4-EVAH!), where were the pictures of John Bridegroom, John Newdad, or even John Gottabaldspot? Where the hell were *those?*

Shrugging, I reached for the bedcover, a soft gray thing whose fabric fell apart like wet tissue as I tried to pull it from the bed.

When I looked at it again, the bedspread had changed. Not gray now, but navy blue, thick and warm. Beneath it lay an older woman sleeping.

No. Not sleeping. Weeping. The woman was *weeping* beneath the blue blanket, her face hidden in the hoodie she'd worn the day she'd taken her son to the forest of West Virginia with its dappled green light, to the hollows where sulfur-yellow masses of chicken-of-the-woods grew on fallen logs of oak, and gray-brown turkey tails fanned up and down the trees.

She'd worn the hoodie on her birthday when he'd brought her the present he'd made for her in senior art class, and it was

the last present from him ever ever

a gray clay pot shaped like a mushroom, a wide-capped trichloma whose gills he'd carefully etched with a toothpick. On one side, the pot held an impression of her boy's fingerprint, one he'd not smoothed out before he fired it, and

fucking car that fucking car

he never wanted a car no gas guzzlers for me mom

just a bike i'll stay in the bike lane

i have a mirror and a helmet and a go pro

i'll be fine

and the woman put her finger on it, *we* put *our* finger on it, and I heard the boy's rueful apology for the fingerprint, but she laughed and said she loved the clay pot even more now exactly because of that, but it *died* the boy died, the plant died the hand her hand our hand dropped from the gray clay pot and the blue blanket felt like the only safe soft place, wet and dark with our weeping, and all around us lay the airless dark in some hidden place of angles and dry earth.

I understood why I'd seen no pictures of John Bridegroom or John Newdad. And why I never would.

i'll stay in the bike lane. i'll be fine.

that fucking car.

The loss and loneliness of the house on Avirosa overwhelmed me then. Standing in that bedroom with its stale air and forgotten photos, I felt the ceaseless layering of day on day on day, each one without him.

It began right after that, I knew. The hoarding. She couldn't lose anything more, that was all. She just couldn't lose more after losing all she had. Her good, sweet boy.

John, yes. That had been his name. But she had called him Jack.

"Hey," came a voice behind me. Abruptly I turned, seeing Imani at the door, her face drawn down in worry. "You okay in there, Paul? You don't look so good."

I blinked. In my hand — I didn't know how — I held a picture, Jack and the gray-haired woman standing beside a tent in a dapple-green forest of West Virginia. "No, I'm —" I began. "I'm fine. It's all fine. No, I'm only —"

Imani looked at me more closely, dark eyes narrowing. "You stood like that for twenty minutes, Paul. I saw you there when I was taking some bags out to the bin. Every time I passed by the door you were there. You ... well, you didn't move. Like, at all. Not even your hand. Or the picture." She nodded at it. "You feeling all right?"

I blinked, touched by her kindness. "I — I don't know. Maybe I need to get some rest? I slept like shit last night." Feeling awkward, I started taking the high school pictures off the wall, trying not to tear them.

"I appreciate your being careful," Imani said slowly, watching me. "But you really don't have to be. The owner doesn't want this stuff, and the woman ... well." She shrugged. "It doesn't sound like she'll need much." She gave me another concerned look and said, "When you're done, why don't you call it a day? Go get some rest."

With that, she turned away and yelled at Kevin to get a move on.

You can't keep everything. You can't even try. I put the picture on the pile and carried it to the dumpster.

But when I opened the desk drawer that once belonged to Jack and found the clay pot he'd made for his mother, I held the thing a long time, feeling its careful contours, seeing the green light of West Virginia, and smelling the echoes of the rich, dark soil still clinging to the curves of fired clay. Finally, I fit my finger in the place he'd left his print.

And I kept it. Right next to the hedgehog cup.

V

The question is not what you look at, but what you see.

Henry David Thoreau

Here's a fun fact. Outside the animal kingdom, our closest relatives are fungi. We share 30-50% of our DNA with them, if you didn't know. That portobello on your salad? It's a literal relative.

Don't worry about this minor act of cannibalism, though. The job of fungi, including salad mushrooms, is to break down dead things and return their nutrients to the soil for repurposing. This includes you. Your lunch is just a temporary loan, a momentary reallocation of molecules. In the end, when you die, the fungi will get it all back. They get everything back. With interest.

You might also not know fungi are intelligent. No, they probably can't do calculus, but they do reason. They make choices. They communicate. They intentionally redirect resources to areas of need.

And like us, they seek connection. Fungi work their way into the very cells of plants around them or dig down into the soil, connecting trees and roots and bushes in a neural and nutritional network called the mycelium — or as some wit named it, the Wood Wide Web. The world's largest living organism is a mycelium that lives in Oregon. It started growing long before Jesus was born.

And it works like a vast subterranean brain.

This is where things get weird.

The next morning, I woke up more tired than I'd been the night before, my mind flat and lifeless as a punctured balloon. About then, I realized I'd been changing. A lot.

I took a shower with my eyes closed. Even on a cursory examination, I found more weird flesh projections had sprung up practically overnight. I touched the growths, sensitive as newborn baby fingers, tiny human roots poking through the top of my scalp, my back, the sides of my feet like pointed pinky toes. Sitting down on the floor of the shower, I worked tentatively at one of the ... projections? Growths? Warts?

hyphae they are called hyphae and i think some are fruiting bodies

springing out at a right angle from my big toe, pushing hard at the base of the stubborn skin prong and wondering if it would simply snap off like the end of a carrot. Instead, pushing on it felt exquisitely painful, and I had to let it be.

Fuck.

You may wonder why I didn't go to the hospital or something. Sure. The hospital. Wonderful place for broken legs, sudden chest pain, and skin carrots. Of course, like everyone else, my health insurance was nominal at best. I could only afford the "budget-conscious, flexible, quality coverage" option, meaning I'd pay a thousand-dollar deductible for a single emergency room visit. For it to be worthwhile, I'd have to be dying. And if I were dying, then what would be the point of going there at all?

Ah, you say, but what about Fast Care?

Sure. Fast Care would be a far better option. Keep me sitting in the lobby for hours before I forked over fifty bucks to hear a bored nurse's assistant tell me I'd caught a case of warts. Maybe send me off with an economy-sized bottle of Compound W or have a doctor dip me in liquid nitrogen until my dick fell off.

Besides, I had no idea how many growths there were. Under the sink, I kept a mirror Derek had used for shaving his neck, and I held it up for a good look at my back.

The fungus had sprung up everywhere.

Tiny baby prongs crept down the ridges of my spine like fleshy push pins. Between my shoulders, where yesterday it had itched like a monster, that cottony filament wove through a hundred human carrots poking curiously from my back like eyes on an old potato. Around my left nipple grew a tiny fairy ring.

This seemed bad. But what if this wasn't the end of it? What if the growths randomly started to do whatever mushrooms did and shot out seeds or sprouts or whatever they did to reproduce?

spores, they use spores, they are so pretty

And what about me? I vaguely recalled seeing a horrifying video about a spider colonized by some invasive fungus that sprouted long white shoots straight out of its head before turning it into a zombie or some shit. Whereas I didn't think Living Dead Paul lay in my future, I had no idea what the hell I should do now. You see, where I'd first found that webwork — yeah, folks, right behind my sac — I could now feel a somewhat larger growth.

This was, in a word, disturbing.

I'd noticed it yesterday when I'd taken off my coveralls after work, thankful every day was Tyvek Day, and I didn't have to worry about the growth I'd felt being visible through my pants. I could only imagine Elisa cracking her gum and saying, "Hey, Paul, is that a load in your undies, or are you just glad to see me?"

At that point, the thing behind my balls had felt like a blister, one of those painless, mushy ones you get on the back of your heel if your shoes are too loose or you wear cotton socks in the summer, so I hadn't given it a lot of thought. After work, though, I'd poked a finger back there hoping I'd feel something normal, like a zit, but no. It was definitely a blister. And yeah, normally I would have grabbed Derek's shaving mirror and given my taint a friendly peek, but I'd been too damn tired after work. Like we all do at one point or another, I put it off until morning, hoping the issue would simply resolve itself overnight. This sometimes happens.

But not this time. No such luck. The blister thing had grown much bigger.

Leaning against the shower wall, I rolled my fingers across the pillow of fluid, feeling something fleshy like a wad of chewing gum inside a leathery membrane. I sighed. Seriously. What the fuck was I supposed to do? For a moment I just stood there letting the warm water course over my back and thought, *Good. Give the plants a water.*

Then came the thought in that low voice.

o no paul they're not plants no not plants at all

completely different kingdom from plantae

though many mushrooms such as those in the amanitaceae family can form an ectomycorrhizal relationship with species such as ...

I groaned. Sticking my face beneath the flow, I turned the shower to cold and stayed there until my head cleared. Jesus. I was turning into a fucking human terrarium, and I was hearing voices.

I think I first heard the voices after Kevin called me to the

Shroom Room, but ever since, they'd only grown stronger. My brain locked onto them like an old transistor radio finding a signal, and now the murmurs played in a warm consistent hum almost below the level of perception. Sometimes the murmuring would focus, and I would hear words. Commentary. Fun fungus facts.

And along with the voices came … pictures. Flashes. Images. Kissing an infant on his face and taking in the milkpure scent of baby breath. Twirling around and around with a brown-haired child on a tree swing. Kneeling in the soil to probe a mushroom that, to my eyes, looked like a slimy brown dick head.

yes paul linnaeus thought it looked like a slimy brown dick head too

the latin term for it is phallus impudicus and they ooze slime to attract flies and the gleba produce methanethiol

And all about us shone the gold-green forest light of West Virginia where the mushrooms grew in the dark, rich soil of fallen trees and leaves.

yes, you should see it paul the moss grows on the rocks like soft green velvet

But most often, and most disturbingly, I kept seeing this: a pressed-in space of corners and angles and no light at all. The sun blotted out, all light extinguished, nothing existing but pressure, pain, and not a breath of air. And oh god, the loneliness. The hours and hours alone. So fucking alone.

Then I remembered when I'd woken at three a.m. last night, I'd been dreaming of crying at the beach. Tears scalded my cheeks like acid, burned my eyes to coals, and I was drowning in waves that tasted like weeping. Half-awake, I reached to the empty side of the bed, feeling only the cold silence of clean sheets.

Then something touched my fingers in the darkness. Took my

41

hand.

So warm.

I'd eased back into sleep, imagining our fingers twining together like thin roots.

By the time I got to 982 Avirosa Avenue that final day, I was several hours late. I'd had more trouble after my morning shower. When Kevin spotted me getting out of my truck, he grunted, "'Bout fuckin' time, man," but when I mounted the stairs with visible effort, my legs spraddled wide like an old buckaroo, Kevin's forehead furrowed with concern. "You all right, brother?" he asked, cocking his chin at me.

"Yeah," I said, trying to sound casually unconcerned, and made up some ridiculous lie about leg day at the gym, grateful the N95 I wore hid the cold pain-sweats on my upper lip. As I passed inside the house, Kevin gave me a gentle slap on the back. He meant well, but god, it hurt like fuck because he knocked off a skin carrot or two. I felt something snap, anyway.

"Nice of you to join us." Elisa sat on the back patio having herself a vape and when she blew out, it reminded me of the spore cloud rising from a pile of books. Despite the pain from Kevin's well-meant slap, I stopped to marvel at the work we'd done. I could see all the way to the walls now, an uninterrupted line of sight from the kitchen to the rooms beyond. The dumpster outside stood brimming.

"Guess what else, though?" said Elisa. "We got some trouble from that fuckin' guy."

I glanced at Imani, sitting in a battered lawn chair. Though I pretty much knew what Elisa meant, I had to ask. "What fucking guy?"

"The homeowner." Imani nodded at the cell in her thin, strong hand. "The brother-in-law. I just got off the phone with him. Right now, the guy's out of town, but he says he's coming back tomorrow afternoon."

I shrugged. "Okay ... so? I mean, we've busted our asses. Anyone can see that. We've cleared out damn near everything — the master bedroom, the kid's bedroom, the bathroom — everything besides the kitchen, right? I mean — " I gestured to the empty house at my back.

"That's not the problem. Well, besides the condition of the house being much worse than he told us." Imani sighed. "You've seen the dumpster. The problem is that right before the client signed off, he gave me one of those 'Oh, by the ways.' As in, 'Oh, by the way, did you happen to see her?'"

"Happen to see who?" I frowned.

"Happen to see the woman who lives here. The biologist lady."

Elisa shook her head and took another drag. "I don't get it. What's he mean, 'if we seen her?' She ain't *been* here. Wasn't she visiting someone or some shit?"

Imani scrolled through her messages. "Here," she said, and passed the phone around, and of course it confirmed everything she'd told us from the start. Clean the house. Clear out the piles. The woman would be visiting friends and moving to assisted living after she returned. Get done before then. "So yeah," Imani said. "Now he wants to know if we've seen her."

"How? How could we have seen her? It's only fuckin' *Wednesday*." Elisa threw up her hands in frustration. "Good thing you handle the calls, Imani, because this dude sounds like a little bitch."

After a minute, Kevin poked his head out the back. "Guys. Her car's still here."

We followed Kevin through the kitchen, and when he opened

the garage door, we saw her car as promised, one of those boxy Jeepy things which had seen a mud road or two in its time. It even looked operational.

"Anyone have the key?" I looked around.

Snorting, Elisa moved past me. "That's an old-ass Land Rover. You don't need a key." When she pulled on the door handle, a litter of fast-food bags tumbled onto the oil-spotted concrete floor, but otherwise, the car was empty. No luggage on the seats, no printouts for flights, no helpful maps, no notes. Nothing.

"Well," said Kevin. "She sure as hell didn't drive herself to the airport." He shrugged, but Imani looked troubled.

Elisa broke the silence. "So? What's the problem? Old mama called an Uber or took a shuttle or something. Smart idea. The long-term parking fee down there is some kind of bullshit. Ten bucks a fuckin' day."

"Yeah, maybe." Imani's troubled look didn't leave. "The thing is, the lady was supposed to be taking a flight to West Virginia."

"So?" Elisa asked again.

"So according to the client ... she never arrived. Nobody's seen her. She didn't make the flight."

The car sat in the garage, blank and unrevealing. If she'd gone, then she'd taken all her things with her, right?

Imani had the same idea. "What about her stuff? Kevin, did we check the trunk for her luggage? Her purse?"

"Her purse? Oh, shit." Kevin looked stricken. "Her — shit. I almost stepped on a purse the day we started, right by the sliding-glass door. I kicked it behind the sofa by the wall 'cause I was afraid we'd toss it out by mistake. Didn't think of it again till two seconds ago."

We all looked at each other, knowing what this meant. Sure, the woman might've left the car behind in her garage because she'd taken an Uber. She might've left a million things we'd never notice because we didn't know her. But almost no one leaves on a trip without their wallet or their pack — or whatever passes for a purse.

"I'll get the purse," I said. It was exactly where Kevin told us it would be.

My second surprise came later. Since the phone call from the homeowner, we'd busted ass to clear any remaining clutter. Fortunately, the science lady hadn't been the kind of hoarder who fills up her vehicle, unlike lots of folks, and the rest of the garage hadn't been bad at all. A hand-operated lawn mower. Some basic Sears tools. Trash bags, metal shelving. Nothing unusual. Still, the kitchen needed doing, and worse, we hadn't found any clues to her whereabouts.

Imani had texted the client to the effect that no, we hadn't seen the biologist lady, but we'd found her purse. Laying the things in front of her while she talked, Imani sent pictures of the contents — an expired driver's license, a half-empty packet of Kleenex, a wrinkled face mask, a paperback book (*We Have Always Lived in the Castle*), a broken-toothed comb with a few silver hairs, a hand-written letter, and the printout with her flight information to West Virginia.

And her wallet.

"Fuck," said Elisa, staring at the purse pile. We'd taken turns reading the letter, hoping for clues. As for me, I wasn't sure it was a letter. I thought it might be a diary.

I've been thinking about what kind of substrate to use, it began. *With the increased proportion of calcium phosphates and carbonate and sodium from the remains, it will be necessary to correct for —*

… He liked Pleurotus djamor best. Said they looked like the

45

flowing skirts of dancers. I saw some — and here the letter had been torn at one corner, as if it had been ripped out of a notebook in haste — *layacapan in Mexico in the mercado there — tart them before the trip in the fruiting chamber and —*

Below, in different ink, the writing on the torn-out page became larger, more erratic.

> *Ted called this AM and I just can't I shouldn't pick up the phone when it's him I know I shouldn't, can't have him over here to see ... to see ... anyway, need to call Ted back and tell him no no no I will not leave the house not now not yet not yet no he's still here he's still here god why will he not let me grieve because he's still no I maybe later not now I can't. Not until he's —*

"Anyone know what to make of this?" Imani asked, holding the letter out to me.

Something scratched at my mind. Along my back. A silent thrumming started up beneath my skin. Then as I held the letter, I saw what she had meant, the images she had thought of:

a clean plastic tub of pink mushrooms flowering from bricks of clean sawdust,

spreading and opening in the air like flowers of salmon like the skirts of whirling dancers, he said.

he'd liked them for their taste, yes.

but mostly for their beauty, frail and transient.

as he had been himself.

Then I blinked.

"No," I said. "No. Not really."

Along the back wall of the kitchen lay stacks and stacks of academic journals. Like the books in the Shroom Room, these journals were coated with the white webwork

mycelial network characteristic of filamental fungi

growing everywhere. Even through my gloves I could feel it, fine and soft as baby hair, thrumming like a wire. I picked up the top copy of *Mycopathologia Quarterly*, and idly thumbed through a 2015 university study on keratinolytic enzymes as a virulence factor for dermatomycoses and read halfway through it before realizing I understood it as effortlessly as if it were a Buzzfeed quiz about "Which Fast Food Nugget Are You?"
Dermatomycoses. Fancy word for skin fungus. Very relatable content.

Very.

Next to Elisa in the kitchen, I worked faster to make up for the time I'd lost in getting to the house so late. Especially since we'd found the woman's purse, I felt a pressing sense of urgency, of wild imbalance, a badgerlike feeling urging me to dig, to unearth, to clean, to clear, to find. Find what? I didn't know. I needed to. I just needed to, that's all.

Also, something was very wrong with me.

Before I'd been stable enough to drive, I'd had to wait until the pain between my legs had died down to a dull maroon roar. Now, as I bent and heaved and lifted, the taint blister flared up again. I pinched my lips to a narrow line, grateful Elisa couldn't see because she'd only make a joke about how I shouldn't be nutting so hard or something. While this wasn't the problem, it touched too close to the truth.

I suppose I should've been glad the trouble I'm talking about began when I was sitting on my couch drinking my morning coffee. Behind the wheel on the interstate would have been infinitely worse. Probably fatal. Certainly inexplicable.

After my shower I'd dressed gingerly, easing my largest, softest t-shirt carefully over what I thought of as my spinal terrarium, especially the little prongs in back. I already wore sweatpants usually saved for Thanksgiving afternoon, and otherwise, I'd decided to go commando. The less elastic rubbing against my skin, the better. Maybe the air flow around my business would — I didn't know. Dry things up, maybe.

As I stared at the spinal prongs reflected in Derek's old shaving mirror, my eyes couldn't quite make sense of the image. I'd spent hours last night googling information on skin growths, everything from lipomas to seborrheic keratoses, but nothing matched. Finally, I typed in "skin carrots," but this didn't help either, and a few searches led to what you could call "highly niche" sites on OnlyFans.

The more you know.

On the plus side, my hands were getting better, and on my face and neck, the growths had almost all fallen off. Thank god. I didn't understand why those more exposed growths had decided to see themselves out the door, but I had a vague suspicion the fungi preferred growing in places that felt moist and dark and warm. You know, like the back of my balls.

When I bent for my sock, I must have put too much pressure on that blistery growth down there, the one covered with the leathery membrane, because as I leaned over, I felt something release with a quiet pop. Immediately, the bottom of my sweats darkened with fluid, and the smell, foul as old pus, filled the room with the yellow-amber reek of fleshy rot.

Hissing with the sting of it, I yanked off my sweats and sat on my floor in a patch of sunlight to see what was going on, futilely wishing I'd decided to take yoga so I could do this without pulling a tendon. Bending around myself like a dead spider and praying no neighbors could see into my window, I reached down with one tentative finger between my legs to get a sense of what had just happened. *Christ. I hope my nuts didn't explode or something,* I thought, but my guys were reasonably fine.

Behind my balls, though, all was not well. Not at all.

Behind my balls, something rooted inside me was trying to come out.

It felt like a baby hand. Just a tiny baby hand with fingers all pinched together like someone making the classic gesture for money, baby fingers with teeny tippy-tips sharp and definite as claws.

I think I moaned something like *no no no no no* and braced my foot on the coffee table to get a better view, some angle that might put this all into perspective. *How about some positive affirmations there, Paul?* I told myself. How about, *Oh, it's just a pimple,* or even, *It's actually much smaller than I thought.*

When I tried to shove my sac to one side, the baby fingers moved.

Then they bit me.

I don't really remember everything from the next few seconds — there's a permanent blank spot in my memory labeled "WHAT THE ACTUAL FUCK" — but I recall my breath coming in harsh pants like *hunnngh, hunnngh, huhhhh, hunnn* as I staggered down the hall toward the bathroom, my sweats pooling around one ankle and streaking amber smears behind me on the tile.

With Derek's mirror in hand, I stumbled back to the sun patch and sat down, trying to position the glass between my legs for a better view of that no-man's land between balls and asshole my college roommate had called a guiche and my brother Pete and I had simply termed the taint. Since I didn't look at this area very often, it took me more than a second of awkward, painful fumbling before the image appeared in the mirror.

Then I saw it, and my mind again refused to process what I was seeing.

It was   It was impossible, you see, because
          The things were
          The things down there were bright red prongs.

Three long scarlet fingers slowly slid out into the world, emerging from that blistery sac behind my balls to spread out in the sunlight like a flower made of crab claws.

Octopus tentacles they look like octopus tentacles o shit o shit I have an octopussy now what now what.

Studded with dark, inky spots, the finger tentacles waved and curled backward on themselves, orchid-like, the projections lightly tickling the hair on the inside of my thighs like a careful seducer of virgins. *Come here, loverboy, I promise it won't hurt.*

And in the middle. Oh, god, in the smack middle of the flowering flowerthing, what the fuck. A mouth yawned open in the center, a tiny green-white circle full of pointed fish teeth.

I don't remember the next few moments, not quite. Memories come only in brief flashes like strobe lights in a nightclub.

I may have screamed. I probably did, because I heard a high-pitched sound cycling up and down like an alarm, and in the back of my mind I thought, *Oh, how delightful. Derek's making tea and the water's boiling yes of course I'd love a cup of earl grey* as the shrieking went on and on. I scuttled back from the window (*crab-walk time, ha ha*), and kicked at the mirror, absurdly thinking that somehow I'd — I don't know, leave the monstrous guichegrowth behind if I shoved its reflection away with my heels.

I felt it moving, gently waving as if caressed by currents of an invisible ocean, the red fingers stroking my skin, tickling the hair there (*loverboy come here loverboy ooooohhhhh loverboy*), and in my horror, I threw myself to the floor and reached between my legs until I felt the tentacles in my hand, long and somewhat leathery, but soft and yielding. One of the growths squirmed inside my palm and I screamed some more, and in a blind rush of terror over-shadowing even the panicked voice of reason warning me, *Hey, Paul, don't pull off your own dick by mistake; you might need it later for something*, I started yanking at anything that moved. I was far, far beyond the ability to reason or care.

When I came back to myself, my hand was stuck to the floor with my own blood. From my navel on down, streaks of yellowish-rust the color of weak iodine clung to my skin and tamped my hairs down flat, and with a horrified gasp of recollection, I grabbed my crotch, assuming the worst and unable to understand what the worst might be.

Miraculously, my dick and balls were still hanging around like always, and the relief felt so palpable I cried. Good boys. Good staying.

But beside me lay a mess of scattered bits and pieces, chunks of claw with dark red ends tipped with triangles like fingernails and insides white as the flesh of cooked crab.

I shoved myself back instinctively, butt-scooting to a safer dis-tance from the chunks of ballsack clawthings, but I really didn't have to. The pieces looked small and insignificant as they lay there dehydrating in a shattered, scattered mess upon the floor, a little sad, a little broken.

Slowly, I moved a finger near a piece of clawthing and waited for it to react, but it didn't. I picked it up, tweezing it between fin-gers and thumb and laying it out on my palm so I could get a closer look at it.

Then it twitched.

I let out another squawk and flung the piece of clawthing away, thinking of the summer my uncle Eddie brought over a rattlesnake he'd shot in the desert behind his house. He'd taken the decapitated snake out of his old green ammo bag and laid it on the driveway for Pete and me to look at. Though it had no head, the body rolled and twisted when either of us touched it, furious to bite and bite us with its empty throat.

But I wasn't sure about the tentacle I'd thrown.

After a minute, I found it near the wall and picked it up again. At the touch of my hand, the clawthing curled into an apologetic spiral as if trying to make itself smaller, less offensive. *I'm sorry*, it seemed to say. *I was just trying to feel the sun.*

All around me in my ears and in my head, I heard the soft and murmurous voices, or maybe one single voice overlapping, gentle and soothing, almost crooning, almost weeping.

> *so sorry paul poor paul my god my poor boy paul*
> *oh so sorry that must have been so unexpected it meant no harm*
> *but how were you to know oh poor paul*

In the end, the only thing that made me feel better was lying in that sun patch. I kicked my foul sweats away and gathered up the shredded bits of finger tentacle on the floor, not sure what to do with them. I held them in my palm, but none of them moved or curled up anymore. When I washed them down the drain in the kitchen sink, I felt a stab of guilt, a flannel shirt guilt, a lost soul doll guilt.

Fuck.

You can't keep everything, my brother had told me. *You just can't.* But increasingly, it seemed as if I couldn't keep anything.

Naked as a child, I curled inside the rectangle of sun and settled for hours in the goldenlit warmth, moving along the floor with the light like our old family cat used to do. Finally, the beam crept up the wall, the living room dimmed, and the roaring pain in my crotch had quieted to a dull throb.

Of course I thought of going to the Fast Care, or maybe to the emergency room for a thousand-dollar visit regarding taint fingers. Sure. I'd been bleeding, not a lot, not more than a few epic nose-gushers I've had in my life, but still. More concerning was the blown-out blister balloon behind my balls, and apart from worrying about an infection, I wasn't certain I could still pee normally or have children.

Had I just *had* children?

In the end, I didn't go to either one. Can you imagine the questions? Or the bill? What I needed more were answers. God, did I ever need answers. I needed them badly enough to dig out a clean pair of non-bloody sweats from my closet and drive to 982 Avirosa Avenue, an old bar towel pinned between my legs like a DIY diaper.

982 Avirosa. Wherever the answers were, I'd find them there. I had to.

VI

The smallest sprout shows there is really no death ...
All goes onward and outward, nothing collapses,
And to die is different from what anyone supposed, and luckier.

Walt Whitman

We were in the kitchen clearing out the last of the stuff. We'd have to rent an additional dumpster, the forty-footer having long since been filled, but at least we'd be done by Thursday before the client got back. Imani had texted back and forth with him about the scientist lady, but after she asked if the police should be notified about a missing person or whether a report should be filled out, she hadn't heard back from him. "Maybe he's out of cell range," Imani said, putting the phone in her pocket after checking it a tenth time.

Elisa snorted. "Or maybe he's an asshole. Probably hopes the lady'll up and die so's he can have the house and won't have to pay any assisted living fee."

"Hey, that shit's expensive," Kevin said, shrugging. "My uncle had to sell his new car to pay for it."

"Fuck you, Kevin. It's his *family*, man. I've got no sympathy for that asshole." Elisa shook her head. "None."

I didn't say anything. To be fair, I saw Kevin's point. When our mom got sick, both Pete and I had done some grim number-crunching about the cost of care, and it was ugly, to say the least. "We'll probably have to put her house on the market," Pete told me. "Make a bunch of healthcare CEOs even richer." As it turned out, Mom died before that happened, but what Pete and I were never going to talk about for as long as we lived was my bitter flash of gratitude in knowing we wouldn't have to cash in our family home after all.

Still, I thought Elisa had it right. The guy had been an asshole. At the end of your life, what matters more than the connections you've made, the others you've loved? What else are you left with? If nothing else, cleaning hoarder houses had taught me that the motto *He who dies with the most toys wins* was just a bunch of sad and empty bullshit. Still, I had to wonder. What connections did the lady have left? Once her son had died, she had become … well, rootless.

I thought of Mom, of how the cleaned-up house echoed with-out her things in it. Of how my life echoed without her in it. Of Pete, wrapped up in the life he'd built with his wife, his kids. I followed him on Instagram. I thought of Derek, who'd found me too empty and messy and sad. Of reaching out to feel the cold, unwrinkled sheets on his side of the bed. Of how I'd come to feel untethered somehow, as if I might be blown away.

Rootless. Yeah.

I could relate.

One line from the woman's letter kept floating through my head at odd moments, the bit about … *need to call Ted back and tell him no no no I will not leave not yet not yet no he's still here I he's still no I maybe later not now I can't. Not until he's* — I didn't know what it meant, exactly, but it didn't take Mulder and Scully to figure out the identity of the mysterious "Ted" — or decipher what she meant by saying *I will not leave not yet.*

Imani understood that all too well. In her years cleaning places containing various degrees of hoard, she had witnessed more than enough grieving folks torn from their rotting, tumbledown houses by well-meaning relatives who hoped to cure their mom's or uncle's or grandpa's hoarding by hiring a professional cleaning team.

Imani wouldn't take those jobs anymore, the ones where the tenant hung around. They'd become far too painful for her and for them, grieving as their world got thrown away. Most wept and wept, clinging to discarded water bottles, unpaid electric bills, plastic FroYo spoons, a dead dog's collar, HBO Guides, flannel shirts, clay pots. Little china cups. Trash, maybe, but sometimes trash is all you have to cling to. All you have left to love.

What else had the lady's letter said? *He's still here I he's still ...* I thought of the faded blue blanket and the little clay pot. *He's still here.*

Yes. *He's still here.* I thought I understood that part myself.

"Oh, shit," said Elisa.

I looked over. Behind the box Elisa had just moved, a big one tucked into an awkward juncture between the water heater and the fridge, we spotted a door we'd never seen before.

The door was a smallish thing dropped below the level of the kitchen by a step or two, like the one for my grandparents' basement in Maine. Here in the Southwest, basements weren't common. With lots of empty land, folks would rather build side to side than up and down, and besides, it was a pain in the ass to dig through caliche. But Southwest or not, that door could lead to almost nothing else.

"Imani!" Elisa called, then turned back to see if she could open it. She was tough, compact, better than Kevin at using her legs to find the right leverage, but even after bracing her feet on the downward step like for a barbell squat machine, Elisa managed to shove open the door by just an inch or two. Even both of us together didn't move it much more, and by the time we gave up, my crotch had started throbbing again, and I prayed I wasn't bleeding through my Tyvek. By dint of sheer persistence, Elisa pushed it open enough to wedge her shoulder inside, but beyond that point, the door stayed firmly stuck.

"KEVIN!" Elisa strode out of the kitchen, leaving me with my hand on the knob like an awkward traveling salesperson. Rooted in place for the moment, I heard the murmuring voice speak up again in the silence

yes paul yes still here still here

and around me the calm, persistent thrumming grew louder, a sound running beneath my skin like a low-current wire. The pain in my crotch I'd been working through now faded into insignificance, as if murmured away, and my hair stood at attention.

yes yes yes still here still

here paul here

With Imani in tow, Elisa returned and together we gave one more decisive push, hearing the wood of the doorway give a crack. "Interior door," Imani grunted. "Hollow core thing. Damn. It'll probably need to be replaced anyway — really, this whole place is a house flipper's dream — but still, I don't want to be paying for a replacement door, folks, know what I mean?" We did, especially since the client did seem like he'd be the type.

"Can we — I don't know — remove the door or something?" I asked, but Imani shook her head. The hinges were on the other side. Even if we could, the problem was obvious: we weren't really done. The uncertain light of the kitchen told us all we needed to know. We were staring at a basement stairwell choked like a throat with solid hoard.

Imani took a deep breath, reeling back at the odor, the familiar sickly-sweet smell now mixed with the earthy scent of a basement hole.

"Jesus." Kevin took off his hat and dabbed the sweat from his forehead with the back of his sleeve. "Even if we decide to bust open the door, we don't have the space for all this in the dumpster. Not in five dumpsters."

"You said it," said Elisa.

"And we don't have time for this." Imani looked at her watch. "He's going to be here in three hours."

Nothing could be done, so by common accord we decided to take a break. Imani sat on the seat-sprung remains of an old kitchen chair with a pen and some paper trying to work things out while Elisa and Kevin hung around outside and had a smoke. Finally, Imani joined them, hoping for better reception on her cell while she made calls to the dumpster rental, the homeowner, the city, and re-consulted the contract they'd signed. As she'd suspected, it made no mention of any basement on the property.

At last, she clicked her pen closed and sighed. "Bottom line, we don't have the time or the equipment to do this."

"No kidding." Elisa blew a large vape cloud. "Especially not for some asshole who probably thought we'd do it for free."

Elisa had it right. We couldn't do it. All the same, my eyes kept returning to that door, the dark crevice we'd managed to open. Out of seemingly nowhere, I remembered Pete and me in Sunday school. The church lady had given us coloring books and crayons and warned us to keep quiet. Riffling through the coloring book, I came to a page where a sad-faced cartoon Jesus stood before his friend's tomb, weeping.

Take away the stone, Martha.

But Lord, there will be a stench, for he has been dead four days.

Take away the stone.

Something clicked into place. Over the last few nights, I'd seen this space in my dreams a hundred times, the dark maw leading to a darker place of sullen earth and angles all askew.

Lazarus. Lazarus, come forth.

And throughout it grew the white web of mycelium.

My lips went dry, and when I finally spoke, my voice cracked. "Hey. I know this sounds — She's down there. She — the scientist. I think she's down there."

For a moment, the others simply stared, but in the background, I saw Elisa nodding. At first, Imani opened her mouth to make a perfectly reasonable objection like, *Oh, come on, Paul. How could an old lady have gotten the door open all by herself and then moved all this crap back to block the stairs? It's not logical.* She started to speak, and I knew if Imani asked me that or something like it, I had no reasonable answer. Not even one. But I knew it was true. Looking at Imani's face just then, I saw she believed me.

The smell, you know.

Elisa said it first. "Then there's got to be another way inside."

In the end, Kevin found the other basement entrance. With dogged focus, he'd searched the house twice for another door before going outside and trying his luck from a different angle. Then he found a faint dirt track leading from the backyard door, one we hadn't seen beneath the overgrown Bermuda grass and desert broom and dead remains of plants. When we followed the track to its conclusion, we understood why nobody had spotted the door: like the one in the kitchen, this entrance sat just below ground level behind the overgrown bushes I'd puked on.

"Oh, hell no. No way. I'm not going inside there." Kevin's mustache dripped with midafternoon sweat, and he gave it a swipe with the back of his hand. "If she's down there, she's dead as a doornail, and I just can't. Dead woman in a basement? No fuckin' way. I've seen *Psycho* too many times, dude. I'm noping the fuck out of this one." He threw up his hands in surrender.

I nodded. "That's okay. It's all good. No worries."

Kevin drew a bandana from his pocket and rubbed his head, reconsidering. "I suppose she could have got trapped or something, like in an earthquake. I mean ... it hasn't been that long. She might've been able to hold out, right? Wouldn't we have heard her?" We'd both seen the blockage in the stairway, though, stifling all the sound. But not the smell.

"Maybe. I guess," I told him, not believing it. "Anyway, I'm going in. Wish me well." I pulled up my hood, hoping he wouldn't slap my shoulder for good luck and knock off another skin carrot.

"Wait," Kevin reached into his utility belt and after some fumbling, passed me a small headlamp. "You'll need this."

I didn't give myself time to consider it. I took the light and didn't look back.

This door opened easily, as I'd supposed it might, but I couldn't see a thing. A cloud passed over the sun, and the day barely lit a small wedge on the concrete floor. All around me rose the earth scent ... and the stench.

This was the dark place from my dreams.

I flicked on the headlamp.

Around me, lit by the beam, I saw a glowing world of white.

White threads like frozen spiderwebs dangled from every surface from rafters to floor, concealing objects as if under snowfall. I
made out a bike wheel webbed with ghostly spokes, the worn
corner of an Atari console, a taped-up canister of Lincoln Logs.

Backing up, I knocked my hip against an old wood table, and
a small pile rattled down over the layers of junk, spilling out a fat
white lump with staring eyes and a yawning mouth that moved as
if to bite. I jerked away in horrified disgust, dislodging more of the
pile and burying my legs to the knees in crumbling magazines and
rotting clothes. Only then did I realize the moving object was some
stupid animatronic teddy bear, but by then, Kevin was shouting at
me from outside, demanding to know if I needed help.

"I'm good, dude," I called back, but I wasn't. Not at all.

I whispershouted into the darkness of the basement, unnerved
by the unmoving silence of the place. "Hey. Hey. Anybody down
here? You okay?"

No answer came.

Dust danced in the beam of the headlamp. Following the
light, I picked out a path through the hoard. All around, boxes and
bags and forgotten furniture arched over my head, silent and mean.
We will bury you, they seemed to say. *You can spend eternity with a
bike spoke in your heart. We will shroud your moldering corpse in a
plastic contractor's bag. You can rot next to the Lincoln Logs.*

Not wanting to touch anything, I eased to the left, following a
faint outline of tracks leading through the white webwork like
footprints on snow. At last, my beam picked out a surface that
threw my light back into my eyes, a long sheet of translucent

plastic covering a doorway from top to bottom.

Closer up, I understood. The door led to a bathroom, one of those simple affairs you put in if you convert your basement to a game room or a guest room, the kind with just a toilet and sink or maybe a rudimentary shower. But the bathroom would almost certainly have a light, maybe even a functional one. After all, the lights for the rest of the house had worked, so why not these?

From outside, Kevin called again, his voice muted by the looming basement piles. "You doin' okay, Paul?"

"Yeah!" I yelled back. "I'm good!" But once more, the place assumed that patient, pressurized silence, and again, I called, "Anyone here?" to be sure.

Again, no answer came. Only the dark earth-scent and the silent white mycelium. Even the head-sound I'd been calling the murmurs — those random observations, whispers, sighs, mutters, the susurrations of thought and emotion I'd heard in my head almost constantly — had fallen silent also, as if the place itself were holding its breath and waiting. I turned the beams on the mycelium network and felt a ripple of apprehension. From it or from me? I could no longer be sure. Under my skin where the white webwork grew densest, my nerves began to hum and vibrate like plucked strings. Nervous, I drew a deeper breath, and noticed the subtle humidity down here, forest-like and moist above the mineral scent of earth. Beneath it all lingered the sickly-sweet odor that had sent me running from the house to hurl in the bushes until I'd gotten so used to it I didn't even smell it anymore.

Down here the smell seemed stronger. Oh, yes. So much stronger.

Stepping over fallen things, I got to the bathroom at last. The plastic door curtain had been zipped shut, but the headlamp picked out a structural framework inside like a giant plastic tent within the bathroom.

I stepped closer, hearing a steady hum like fans and a small, quiet ticking. Peering into the plastic enclosure, I saw some interior shelving had given way. The sheeting had partly ripped out at the door and the tent floor seemed covered with an irregular brown mass. When I took another step, my toe hit a solid roundish thing, a hand-carved wooden urn of some kind. My fingers gently ran across the wavelike patterns on the surface, its arcs and turnings, so I set the vase inside the bathroom door to keep it safe.

Taking a deep breath, I passed my hand along the interior wall, hoping to encounter a switch plate. In the background, the quiet ticking grew momentarily louder.

Then the room lit up like fire.

Stumbling back, I made some unlovely squawk. I hadn't found a switch plate, so where this light had come from, I had no damned idea. For a second I stood half-blinded, startled as a cave fish at a diver's lamp. Inside the plastic tent, broad strips of fluorescents had just come on by themselves.

"Paul?" Kevin's faraway shout came tinged with genuine worry. "You okay in there, bro?"

"Yeah," I shouted back. "It's all good, Kevin. Sorry. Yeah — got the lights on down here, anyway."

A timer, I thought. The lights had to have been on a timer. Of course, because this wasn't really a bathroom.

It was a growth chamber.

I stepped through the rip in the plastic tent.

For a moment, I stood in awe like a child peering out at a world of warm snow. The mycelium webwork had taken over, whirling across every surface like puffs of dandelion, Siberian frost,

R.A. Busby

or the beautiful white hair of an ancient queen. Inside, the air felt humid, and I recognized a device my college roommate had called a reptile fogger. The room held shelves upon shelves, each stacked with familiar shapes. I found one and rubbed the surface clean. A plastic Sterilite container. Because of course.

And through it all, poking up everywhere like inquisitive parasols, grew mushrooms of every description. White oyster mushrooms spread out like waiter's trays from a batch near my face, heavy with the scent of licorice and fish. Above this grew a round fungus like a Koosh ball with spikes of glacial white. I saw Mario Kart shrooms, angel trumpet things, and one like a sea sponge. On my left grew a cluster of red spikes dangling from a leathery egg casing, and I instantly recognized those as ballsack shrooms. Guichegrowth. Taint tentacles.

In the back of the tent, a shelf had collapsed on the floor, its supports cutting through the protective plastic. All around I saw scattered Sterilite containers, and here the mycelium grew thickest, sprouting on a hillock overgrown with miniature brown shrooms.

Then I noticed the dead woman's hand.

It reached out from a pile of soil and mushrooms, a dark purple starfish, fingers grasping air like a drowning victim. Two of the fingers had gone a dark gray while the others assumed the amber-orange shade of smoked ham. Beside the hand curled gray human hair that mingled with the webwork, spreading toward me like the threads of the mycelium itself.

Well. I guess I found her.

She'd been trying to reach the top containers, I thought. She'd gotten up on a stepstool and tried to brace herself against the shelving when she lost her balance, or the shelf collapsed, or maybe both. Imani had mentioned the woman had fallen before, so maybe she'd felt dizzy, or simply stepped wrong on the stool and over-balanced. Happens all the time. Either way, down she fell along

64

with the shelf, the Sterilites, and the soil. On the smooth curved corner of the bathroom sink near her head, I saw a brownish smear and guessed it might be from her blood.

Yes. She'd fallen, and her head had struck the sink as she fell. I could almost hear it happen. A sharp, solid whack, and then silence.

She never got up after that. Never packed her luggage, never used her plane ticket, never slung her purse over her shoulder, never took that trip. She'd been here the whole time, like soil, like earth, right beneath our feet.

The last thought I had before the lights flickered out was this: *They ate her. The mushrooms escaped from their containers, and they ate her.*

The disaster happened without warning.

I tried to call for Kevin, but my throat had gone dry, my hands clumsy and stuttering, my feet unable to untangle.

I'd never seen a dead body. Not in person. After Mom died, she'd been transported to the mortuary for cremation, and by some unspoken agreement my brother Peter had taken the urn with her ashes. I didn't know what Pete intended to do with it, and I doubt he had any idea either. I just knew I didn't want it. During the service, I couldn't even look at the thing. All that Mom had been could never fit inside that stupid urn.

"Kevin?" I winced as my toe hit the wooden vase for the second time, and I shifted it farther inside for safekeeping. Kevin didn't answer. I gave a louder yell. "Hey, Kev? Kevin, I think we found her, dude. Hey, we need to get emergency services in here, all right, so would you —"

Then came a low rasp of metal against metal, a tired sound of too much weight and time, the exhausted sigh of loss and entropy. From the pile came a crack loud as a gunshot, some final thing reaching the limits of its own structural integrity. For a horrified second, I thought of the Collyer brothers and knew it was a sound they might remember. Then the pile shivered, shifted, and plunged like an avalanche toward me, filling the ground before my feet and obliterating the way I'd come. Killing the light. Trapping me in the room. Trapping me in the dark.

But at least I had company.

The pile blocked the door almost entirely. Moving anything caused terrifying seismic shifts, and I feared if I tried to dig out, I'd get pinned or smothered beneath a stack of academic journals about mycology or maybe get stabbed through the throat by a random bike spoke. I called Kevin until my throat was raw and finally shut up only when I started worrying about oxygen depletion. For now, at least, the best choice seemed to hope the cavalry would come, or Kevin would figure things out, or an emergency crew would show up with the jaws of life. I just had to sit tight.

Here. In the dark. With the dead.

I know why the dark makes us afraid. It is a mirror of our fear. *Come*, it says. *Let me show you the shadows and the things that move within them. Let me show you endings. Let me show you loss.*

Lazarus, come forth.

But Lord, he has been dead four days.

And because the dark is a mirror, I saw vast emptiness that stretched into forever. Nothing existed beyond this sad little flash of life. No heaven, no happy reunions with the ones you loved. Just darkness and loneliness and void.

I don't remember when I started to cry. I'd been doing it for a long time, hours perhaps, the snot trickling down my nose until it hurt to wipe, and I cried because everything besides the dark, the silence, and the abandonment seemed a hollow and faintly ridiculous dream. There had never been a sun. Never been an earth. Never been a kiss or a touch or a love.

I ached. I ached for Derek, for my mother, for my brother, for my world. For anyone.

And for the woman too. Had she felt this too when her eyes fell finally shut? She'd built a fortress of possessions, a labyrinth of volumes and journals, frames and photographs (*CLASS OF '95 4-EVAH*), teacups, Sterilite containers, a sweet art-class pot with her dead son's fingerprint embedded in the clay, her blue blanket and old hoodie, and all of it a monument to memory, a testament to grief. So much grief. So many things, and every thing an absence.

And it had killed her like those old Collyer brothers in their brownstone, and probably killed me too. For nothing.

no not for nothing not for nothing, paul

The voice came, gentle and low, but in that silence, I jerked back, nearly collapsing another shelf of Sterilite containers and mushrooms onto my head. "What the fuck is going on?" I said, wiping my nose again on the wet cuff of my coverall. "Who are you?"

But I knew.

In the silence, I heard the whisper again. *There is no such thing as nothing, Paul. Not for you. Not for me. Not for anyone.*

I shook my head. "I don't understand." Around me drifted the soil-scent, the earthy mushroom webwork, the heavy reek of her decay. My fingers dug into the dirt, gripping it blindly, sensing its reality. "Of course there's nothing." I let out a bitter chuckle. "Look at me."

I am looking at you.   Paul. I am dead. I'm decomposing.

I wiped my nose. "I can tell."

And you will die and decompose one day, as will we all. But don't you understand? All of me is still here. All of it. All the matter making up my bones, my flesh, my brain, the water in my blood, all the air I ever breathed. Each thermal unit of each bit of energy I gave off in my life. Every atom of which I was made. The carbon. The oxygen. The hydrogen. All of it is here, right here on earth with all of us. It always has been.

As I dug my hands into the soil, the webwork thrummed, the fibers twining around my wrists, my fingers, or maybe I twined my fingers into it, because for a second, we seemed to be the same thing. And somehow through that network, I caught the images the woman had been sending clear as a lived moment:

A chunk of ice calving from a giant glacier in summer.

… the glacier floating in the water, a beautiful aquamarine jewel releasing parts of itself into the ocean …

… water rising as bright mist above dark sea to swell the soaring thunderheads above, then falling back to earth as feathered snow and freezing ice …

… and melding to a glacier to be born, risen, and renewed once more.

This is you, she told me. *This is me. This is the great truth the physicists spoke of: Matter cannot be created nor destroyed but only changed.*

"So?"

That means everything you ever loved is here. Nothing has been lost, not one atom in the history of the universe. They are right here. They have never gone away. And Paul? They always will be.

My tears, hot and aching, fell into the soil. *I would never throw you away*, I thought, and I think I meant them all. Everyone. Maybe even me.

I rubbed my stinging eyes. "Are you — I mean, I don't even know who you are."

Don't you?

No, we haven't been formally introduced, I almost said, but the second the words came to mind, I realized they were bullshit.

Cleaning is a profoundly intimate act. Clean someone's house and you will learn them. You will touch what they touched, learn what they read, what they ate, what they showed, what they concealed. What they gave up. What they could never quite let go.

"Yes," I said at last. "Yes, I think I know you."

And I reached out in the darkness and touched those dead gray fingers. Then I held her hand in mine.

VII

One short sleep past, we wake eternally
And Death shall be no more; Death, thou shalt die.

John Donne

It took them a while before they found me. Us. Martha and me.

The shouts and radios of the emergency crew cut through the thick silence before their headlamp beams came dancing up and down the contours of the pile. When I called out, a roar of answering cheers made me tear up again, even though I thought I had no more tears left in me. Cheesy though it sounds, when the first light broke into the room, I started crying again and swiped my eyes with my filthy hands to make sure I really saw it.

Lazarus, come forth.

I did. But by the time that I came forth, I'd been ... transformed.

After everything I've told you, I'm sure you'll understand why I couldn't go on cleaning houses anymore. I sold my half of the business to Imani, and not surprisingly given her smarts and her drive, she's making a real go of it. Elisa and Kevin even started their own Junkitt franchise in the outer 'burbs because the market was so good. They have a company logo and everything.

As for 982 Avirosa, after the city recovered Martha's body, they deemed the house irrecoverable and ordered it torn down. *Well, I do hope Ted gets a decent profit from it,* Martha told me when I drove past the bare lot marking the place she'd lived and died. It took me a minute to remember she meant the brother-in-law who'd wanted to stick her in a nursing home.

I told her that with all due respect, I thought Ted sounded like an asshole. Martha chuckled and said, *No, Paul. He's just a lonely and uncomfortable person, and I was a loose end, his dead brother's wife. He'll be happier now he can sell the property and move on.* Eventually some flippers bought the land and rebuilt the house from scratch, so now the place is kind of pretty, with blooming succulents in front and a mesquite tree in the back that Martha especially liked.

I talk to Martha almost every day. She's always with me, like a stereo playing softly in the background, and often I can hear her laughing with the joy of things — the sunlight through the trees, a frolicking dog catching a frisbee at the park, the rain-like scent of waxy creosote leaves.

Sometimes she'll make wry observations, and the advice she gives is invariably good, especially about what I'll call "personal mushroom management." The skin carrots finally dropped off, and overall, I didn't mind the little bluish pinheads along my spine — they were kind of cute and didn't last long either — but the ball tentacles still concerned me, as I'm sure you understand.

There's no need to be afraid of the ball tentacles. That is, the Clathrus archeri, she said. *Research suggests glycogen synthase* kinase-3 inhibitors like lithium chloride may be used to regulate the development of the fruiting bodies without harming the underlying mycelial network, but Paul ... you could also just pick them when they're little.

I thought of the ruined shards of tentacle dehydrating on my floor, how I'd held one in my hand and watched it curl into a sad little spiral before I threw it away, not knowing what else to do with it. "Yeah. I could," I said. "Or maybe I could just ... let them live."

Why, of course you can. They're part of you.

They were, weren't they? As I was part of them.

Yes. Besides, they are only fruiting bodies, after all. In practical terms, they're not built to last long, so if you don't like them—or their smell when mature—you can pluck them. Or just wait a while. They spring up quickly and they're gone almost as fast, beautiful as flowers and as brief. Like we are. It's the mycelium that lasts forever — or nearly so. Do you want me to show you?

I did.

Then Martha's mind brought me before the oldest living network in the world, a single organic fungal web spread across thousands of acres, thousands of years, yet its memories were older. *Do you want to see them, Paul?* Martha asked, and when I told her yes she held her hand out to me again, and as before, I took it.

And felt the weight of forever.

The network remembered all things, retained all things, preserved all memories of ancient forms before it and passed those down from branch to branch, from year to year, from age to age, a priceless inheritance of mycelial memory stretching back to the beginnings of all life, to the origins of the entire fungal clade.

She let me go and I collapsed. For days, I couldn't move. Couldn't speak. Couldn't form my thoughts in human words.

2.4 billion years is a very long time.

I understand why Martha died. It had been the only way she could preserve him.

Through Martha's eyes, I watched her final moments. She'd been in the plastic-sheeted bathroom, intent on the bag of grain spawn she was shaking into a Sterilite container. Her fingers smoothed the white mushroom spores into the substrate there as if soothing them to sleep, and then at last she held aloft that lovely wooden vase that wasn't really a vase but a funeral urn.

Of all the piles and towers of stuff inside her house, the urn was the dearest thing she had. It was Jack. Or what remained of him.

Bit by bit, she shook the contents of the urn into the bin where it lay on the surface — a dull gray powdered ash speckled with larger bits that looked like kitty litter. Then her fingers dug below into the soil, into the spores, and mingled them. Communion, I thought. This is communion.

I knew I'd have to leave soon, Martha told me. It was my last chance. I wanted to do it before, but I couldn't bring myself to until it was almost too late. He'd wanted to be part of the soil, part of the cycle. He'd wanted to be grown again. Nothing is created or destroyed, Paul. Only changed.

And when the shelves collapsed, her last memory had been of her son's laughing face and his fingerprint on a small gray pot.

I keep this memory. I treasure it in the hoard I hold inside my mind. It is a trove of memories, mine and Martha's, mine and

Jack's, mine and my mother's and her mother's and — well. So many others. All of them. All the living. All the dead. Martha gave those memories to me, entrusted them to me as the richest thing she owned.

Alone in the darkness, I had reached for her hand. And as I touched it, I saw

Everything.

A girl (*me us*) falling into autumn leaves, her (*our*) mouth filled with soil and laughing.

The blue blanket wet against my face in the ticking silence of the lonely house.

The splitpelvis pressure from a baby's round and perfect head emerging into the world, framed by the taut diamond of my flesh around its skull, the slippery release of his shoulders, and the bliss, oh god, the bliss, I love you my sweet boy Jack. I love you my sweet boy Paul.

A little girl looking up to the sky and the amberbrown perfume of leaves in her red hair now turned gray above the shoulders of a worn flannel shirt.

And finally, the dark, the crushing weight, the pain, and the disappearing air ... then mushrooms all around, growing, forming the webwork within me, the spores I'd breathed in taking root inside my flesh, penetrating each cell, my blood and brain and everything. The mushrooms had eaten her, as I'd thought. And she'd been grateful for it.

As I will be.

There came a pause, a hum through the mycelium, the throb of connection, and the thought, *You see, the mycelium is alive, and it remembers. And now ... you do too. You are part of it. Nothing is lost. Everything remains.*

She had given me her life. And now I have given it to you.

74

This story, you understand, is a sort of spore, a tiny living thing shed out into the world. And maybe it will light on you, and you will breathe it in, and you will make it part of who you are.

And you too will speak for the dead.

We've moved back to West Virginia, a place that already seemed familiar before I saw it. All my life, I'd lived in the driest of the dry deserts, a place with a sere and searing beauty all its own, but I was blown away the first time I came north along a branch of the Appalachian Trail that wound down the river gorge to Harper's Ferry. I'd never seen a world so richly green. I touched the soil there in that moss-grown forestland and I knew I had come home.

After a few weeks, I got a decent job working in a warehouse near Bolivar. It's easy enough, mostly stocking pallets, putting things in order, and doing my bit to resist inevitable entropy while driving a forklift and listening to podcasts. It doesn't pay a fortune, but then again, I don't need much. My place is small, close enough to the river to hear its ceaseless conversation if I leave my windows open, and otherwise, there's not much more in my house than space and light.

On the mantel, though, I placed three precious things. The wooden urn. The gray clay pot. The little hedgehog cup. "Are they *your* memories you're keeping, Paul, or *hers?*" my sister-in-law might have asked. The answer is that the memories are ours. And now they are yours too.

On the weekends, I go into the woods. The green silence is full of voices, the chirrups of birds, the chatter of squirrels. I hunt for chicken-of-the-woods or watch the amanitas unfurl their red parasols and the bark of trees sprout fans of turkey tails. And once beneath an oak, I found a rare Astraeus, its outer shell split open in a dark corona ringed around a central puffball. It lay on the earth like a fallen star. In the evenings, I work on an article for one of those journals we unearthed at 982 Avirosa, and maybe it'll be published one day. A surprising amount of mycological research is done by dedicated amateurs like me, foragers or locavores or latter-day hippies who don't always have degrees in biology but who find fungi in the woods and write about them. My particular research focus is on the mycorrhizal potentialities of a human-fungal hybrid.

Relatable content. Very.

And in the woods, I found out you sometimes get to meet people, especially in the places mushrooms grow.

Last week, I spotted him with a group of amateur mycologists I'd found through Meetup. He knelt by a log, carefully positioning his thumbs on either side of a morel cap to check whether it was hollow and edible. It was. When he put it in his bag, I came up and gave a little wave. "Hi," I said. "I'm Paul."

He smiled then, and it lit up his whole face. That was beautiful enough, but it was his hands I noticed first. His fingers, actually. I tend to notice those a lot. It's not a kink; it's just that fingers are perfect. They're like hyphae, those tiny, delicate strands probing through the earth until they find another living thing and make a connection with it, a life twined about with other life. From the well of our isolation, our loneliness, we reach into the dark for those same reasons: for warmth, for compassion. For connection. It begins with our fingers.

And I think his will smell like soil.

Acknowledgments

As always, I would like to thank my family for this work, especially my mother. You could say it began with her.

My mother wasn't a hoarder, but a *placer*. She preferred to put things in one spot and keep them there forever. If they faded or failed, she didn't want to hear about it. As far as she was concerned, entropy didn't exist.

Until she died, I'd never imagined throwing away things like her old grocery lists would be hard, but on my way to the trash can, I realized she'd never make another list again. At that moment, the complex human motivations for hoarding started to make sense to me. What if *nothing* had to be thrown away? What if everything could stay in place forever?

I could relate.

In writing this book, I am deeply grateful to biologist Dr. Merlin Sheldrake, whose work *Entangled Life: How Fungi Make Our Worlds, Change Our Minds, and Shape Our Futures* elegantly lays out the network of relationships all living things share with fungi.

Between his research and that of mycologist Paul Stamets, whose buoyant enthusiasm makes me wish I could take a million bio classes from him, I caught that fascination with these richly varied organisms whose lives are indeed "entangled" with our own.

Through their work and that of others, I came to appreciate that death is not simply an end, but the first stage of renewal—or in the far better words of Walt Whitman, it leads forward life, and does not wait at the end to arrest it. Though the idea for this book began as a single unsettling image—a buried woman's hand reaching out from the darkness—I came to see it not as a moment of horror, but of deepest connection.

Most importantly, I would like to thank Selena Middleton, publisher and editor of Stelliform Press, whose thoughtful suggestions and revisions were invaluable. I will forever be grateful for her time, tremendous patience, and wise expertise, and I hope her garden may forever be filled with portobellos.

In the end, I suspect my mother wished to hold on tight to everything she loved, to preserve the fragile connections we make, to keep everything the same. I understand, and I wish I could tell her this: though everything changes, and everything perishes, nothing is lost.

It's all still here.

It always will be.

About the Author

R. A. Busby is the 2020 Shirley Jackson Award recipient for short fiction, and the author of the horror novella *Corporate Body* (Cemetery Gates, 2023). A member of the Horror Writers Association, R.A. Busby states, "In creative programs, I was always instructed to write about what I know, and I know what scares me." In her spare time, R.A. Busby watches cheesy gothic movies and goes running in the desert with her dog.

YOU MAY ALSO LIKE

these eco-horror titles from Stelliform Press

A World Fantasy Award Finalist, this novella is a twisty, weird, anti-colonial story of a cursed house and the forest goddess who wants it gone.

In the dark rot of an east coast swamp, a queer Mi'kmaw artist is transformed by grief. A new novella by an emerging Indigenous author.

STELLIFORM PRESS

Earth-focused fiction. Stellar stories.
Stelliform.press.

Stelliform Press is shaping conversations about nature and our place within it. We invite you to join the conversation by leaving a comment or review on your favorite social media platform. Find us on the web at www.stelliform.press and on Twitter, Instagram, Facebook @StelliformPress, and Mastodon @StelliformPress@mastodon.online.